AESOP'S FABLES

ILLUSTRATED BY
CHARLES SANTORE

STERLING CHILDREN'S BOOKS
New York

STERLING CHILDREN'S BOOKS
New York

An Imprint of Sterling Publishing
387 Park Avenue South
New York, NY 10016

ISBN 978-1-4027-8412-5

Distributed in Canada by Sterling Publishing
c/o Canadian Manda Group, 165 Dufferin Street
Toronto, Ontario, Canada M6K 3H6
Distributed in the United Kingdom by GMC Distribution Services
Castle Place, 166 High Street, Lewes, East Sussex, England BN7 1XU
Distributed in Australia by Capricorn Link (Australia) Pty. Ltd.
P.O. Box 704, Windsor, NSW 2756, Australia

For information about custom editions, special sales, and premium and corporate purchases,
please contact Sterling Special Sales at 800-805-5489 or specialsales@sterlingpublishing.com.

Printed in Mexico
Lot #:
2 4 6 8 10 9 7 5 3
03/13

www.sterlingpublishing.com/kids

This book is for my mother, Nellie Santore,
in gratitude for passing on to me a precious gift—
the ability to draw.

CHARLES SANTORE

CONTENTS

FOREWORD

Reading through various collections of *Aesop's Fables* with the thought of illustrating a selection of my favorites, I came upon an introduction to an early twentieth-century volume of the fables written by G. K. Chesterton, the great master of English letters. In writing about the animals, Chesterton observed, "They have no choice, they cannot be anything but themselves."

His words were a revelation to me. I could visualize immediately the majestic lion occupying center stage, the shrewd fox sidling up to a situation rather than confronting it directly, the docile sheep forever doomed to plod on, unaware that they are simply pawns in the game of life. I realized that each animal—the worldly wolf, the clever fox, the silly crow—represents some particular aspect of the human condition. Whatever the situation, the animals' reactions resound with familiarity to us—they are predictable. The animals are never more or less than their essential natures, and thus they never disappoint. That is the great essence of each fable.

Ancient as the fables are, they have much to teach our children today. Every child comes to know, for instance, that a tortoise is slow. But the lesson to be learned from the amusing interaction between tortoise and hare in the fable is no less enriching, and no less entertaining, than it was in Aesop's day. The universal truth is that "slow and steady" still wins the race.

I chose to expand on the idea of universality by including fables without humans, thereby avoiding the trappings of time, gender, and geography. Once my choices were made, the illustrations began to crystallize. Each animal, whether wolf, lion, or lamb, needed to convey convincingly—in gesture and in expression—the entire range of human emotions, from fear to arrogance, from stupidity to craftiness, from indifference to affection. Whether or not I have succeeded in this humbling task, well, I will let you, the reader, be the judge.

Charles Santore

THE WOLF
AND THE CRANE

A Wolf once got a bone stuck in his throat: so he went to a Crane and begged her to put her long bill down his throat and pull it out. "I'll make it worth your while," he added. The Crane did as she was asked and got the bone out quite easily. The Wolf thanked her warmly and was just turning away, when she cried, "What about that fee of mine?"

"Well, what about it?" snapped the Wolf, barring his teeth as he spoke. "You can go about boasting that you once put your head into a Wolf's mouth and didn't get it bitten off. What more do you want?"

In serving the wicked, expect no reward,
and be thankful if you escape injury for your pains.

THE WOLF
AND THE LAMB

A Wolf came upon a Lamb straying from the flock and felt some reluctance about taking the life of so helpless a creature without some plausible excuse: so he cast about for a grievance and said at last, "Last year, sir, you grossly insulted me."

"That is impossible, sir," bleated the Lamb, "for I wasn't born then."

"Well," retorted the Wolf, "you feed in my pastures."

"That cannot be," replied the Lamb, "for I have never yet tasted grass."

"You drink from my spring, then," continued the Wolf.

"Indeed, sir," said the poor Lamb, "I have never yet drunk anything but my mother's milk."

"Well, anyhow," said the Wolf, "I'm not going without my dinner," and he sprang upon the Lamb and devoured it without more ado.

Hypocritical speeches are easily seen through.

THE WOLF
IN SHEEP'S CLOTHING

A Wolf resolved to disguise himself in order that he might prey upon a flock of sheep without fear of detection: so he clothed himself in a sheepskin and slipped among the sheep when they were out at pasture. He completely deceived the shepherd, and when the flock was penned for the night, he was shut in with them. But that very night, as it happened, the shepherd, requiring a supply of mutton for the table, laid his hands on the wolf, mistaking him for a sheep, and finished him off with his knife on the spot.

Harm seek, harm find.

THE VAIN JACKDAW

Jupiter, King of the Gods, announced that he intended to appoint a King over the birds, and he named a day on which they were to appear before his throne when he would select the most beautiful of them all to be their ruler. Wishing to look their best on the occasion, they retired to the banks on a stream, where they busied themselves in washing and preening their feathers. The Jackdaw was there along with the rest and realized that, with his ugly plumage, he would have no chance of being chosen as he was: so he waited till they were all gone, and then picked up the most gaudy of the feathers they had dropped and fastened them about his own body, with the result that he looked gayer than any of them. When the appointed day came, the birds assembled before Jupiter's throne; and after passing them in review, he was about to make the Jackdaw King, when all the rest set upon the King-elect, stripped him of his borrowed plumes, and exposed him for the Jackdaw that he was.

Fine feathers do not make fine birds.

THE LION AND THE WILD DONKEY

A Lion and a Wild Donkey went out hunting together: the latter was to run down the prey by his superior speed, and the former would then come up and dispatch it. They met with great success; and when it came to sharing the spoil, the Lion divided it all into three equal portions.

"I will take the first," said he, "because I am king of the beasts; I will also

take the second, because, as your partner, I am entitled to half of what remains; and as for the third—well, unless you give it up to me and take off pretty quickly, the third, believe me, will make you feel very sorry for yourself!"

Might makes right.

THE LION AND THE MOUSE

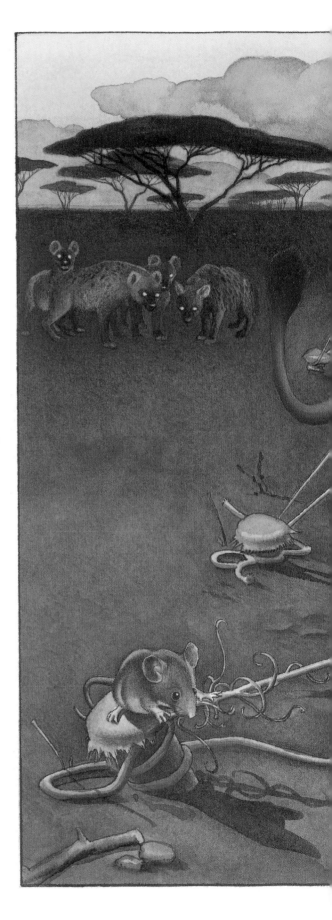

A Lion asleep in his lair was awakened by a Mouse running over his face. Losing his temper, he seized it with his paw and was about to kill it. The Mouse, terrified, piteously entreated him to spare its life.

"Please let me go," it cried, "and one day I will repay you for your kindness." The idea of so insignificant a creature ever being able to do anything for him amused the Lion so much that he laughed aloud and good-humoredly let it go. But the Mouse's chance came, after all.

One day the Lion got entangled in a net which had been spread for game by some hunters, and the Mouse heard and recognized his roars of anger and ran to the spot. Without more ado, it set to work to gnaw the ropes with its teeth and succeeded before long in setting the Lion free.

"There!" said the Mouse. "You laughed at me when I promised I would repay you: but now you see, even a Mouse can help a Lion."

*No act of kindness,
no matter how small, is ever wasted.*

THE DONKEY
IN THE LION'S SKIN

A Donkey found a Lion's skin and dressed himself up in it. Then he went about frightening every one he met, for they all took him to be a Lion, men and beasts alike, and took to their heels when they saw him coming. Elated by the success of his trick, he loudly brayed in triumph. The Fox heard him and recognized him at once for the Donkey he was and said to him, "Oh, my friend, it's you, is it? I, too, should have been afraid if I hadn't heard your voice."

No disguise will hide one's true character.

THE OLD LION AND THE FOX

A Lion, enfeebled by age and no longer able to procure food for himself by force, determined to do so by cunning. Taking himself to a cave, he lay down inside and pretended to be sick; and whenever any of the other animals entered to inquire after his health, he sprang upon them and devoured them. Many lost their lives in this way, till one day a Fox called at the cave and, having a suspicion of the truth, addressed the Lion from outside instead of going

in and asked him how he was. He replied that he was in a very bad way: "But," said he, "why do you stand outside? Pray come in."

"I should have done so," answered the Fox, "if I hadn't noticed that all the footprints point toward the cave and none the other way."

Take warning from the misfortunes of others.

THE MONKEY
AS KING

At a gathering of all the animals the Monkey danced and delighted them so much that they made him their King. The Fox, however, was very much disgusted at the promotion of the Monkey: so having one day found a trap with a piece of meat in it, he took the Monkey there and said to him, "Here is a dainty morsel I have found, sire; I did not take it myself, because I thought it ought to be reserved for you, our King. Will you be pleased to accept it?"

The Monkey went at once for the meat and got caught in the trap. Then he bitterly reproached the Fox for leading him into danger; but the Fox only laughed and said, "Oh, Monkey, you call yourself King of the Beasts and haven't more sense than to be taken in like that!"

A position earned without merit
is as easily lost as gained.

THE FOX
AND THE GRAPES

A hungry Fox saw some fine bunches of Grapes hanging from a vine that was trained along a high tree and did his best to reach them by jumping as high as he could into the air. But it was all in vain, for they were just out of reach: so he gave up trying and walked away with an air of dignity and unconcern, remarking, "I thought those Grapes were ripe, but I see now they are quite sour."

It is easy to despise what you cannot get.

THE WILD BOAR
AND THE FOX

A Wild Boar was engaged in sharpening his tusks upon the trunk of a tree in the forest when a Fox came by and, seeing what he was at, said to him, "Why are you doing that, pray? The huntsmen are not out today, and there are no other dangers at hand that I can see."

"True, my friend," replied the Boar, "but the instant my life is in danger I shall need to use my tusks. There'll be no time to sharpen them then."

Lost time cannot be recalled.

THE FOX
AND THE CROW

A Crow was sitting on a branch of a tree with a piece of cheese in her beak when a Fox observed her and set his wits to work to discover some way of getting the cheese. Coming and standing under the tree he looked up and said, "What a noble bird I see above me! Her beauty is without equal, the hue of her plumage exquisite. If only her voice is as sweet as her looks are fair, she ought without doubt to be Queen of the Birds."

The Crow was hugely flattered by this, and just to show the Fox that she could sing, she gave a loud caw. Down came the cheese, of course, and the Fox, snatching it up, said, "You have a voice, madam, I see: what you want is wits."

Do not trust flatterers.

THE CROW
AND THE SWAN

A Crow was filled with envy on seeing the beautiful white plumage of a Swan and thought it was due to the water in which the Swan constantly bathed and swam. So he left the neighborhood of the inns, where he got his living by taking bits of meat left from the plates of the diners, and went and lived among the pools and streams. But though he bathed and washed his feathers many times a day, he didn't make them any whiter and at last he died of hunger into the bargain.

You may change your habits but not your nature.

THE EAGLE
AND THE CROW

One day a Crow saw an Eagle swoop down on a Lamb and carry it aloft in its talons.

"My word," said the Crow, "I'll do that myself."

So it flew high up into the air and then came shooting down with a great whirring of wings on to the back of a big Ram, with the intention of carrying it off. It had no sooner alighted, than its claws got caught fast in the wool, and nothing it could do was of any use: there it stuck, flapping away and only making things worse instead of better.

By and by up came the Shepherd. "Oh," he said, "so that's what you'd be doing, is it?" And he took the Crow and clipped its wings and carried it home to his children. It looked so odd that they didn't know what to make of it.

"What sort of bird is it, Father?" they asked.

"It's a Crow," he replied, "and nothing but a Crow: but it wants to be taken for an Eagle."

Thoughtless imitation will end in danger.

THE TWO GOATS

Two proud Goats happened to meet on the opposite cliffs of a high mountain range where a fierce river ran below through a rocky valley. The only bridge across the chasm was a fallen tree so narrow as to frighten two mice passing each other at the same time. Both stubborn Goats felt that they had the right to cross the river first; so setting one hoof at a time upon the slender log, they found themselves head to head in the middle of the bridge. Neither Goat would give way to the other, and finally they both fell headlong into the roaring waters below.

It is better to yield than to come to misfortune through stubbornness.

THE TORTOISE
AND THE EAGLE

A Tortoise, discontented with his lowly life and envious of the birds he saw enjoying themselves in the air, begged an Eagle to teach him to fly. The Eagle protested that it was idle for him to try, as nature had not provided him with wings; but the Tortoise pressed him with entreaties and promises of treasure, insisting that it could only be a question of learning the craft of the air: so at length the Eagle consented to do the best he could for him and picked him up in his talons. Soaring with him to a great height in the sky he then let him go, and the wretched Tortoise fell headlong into the sea.

If men had all they wished,
they would often be ruined.

THE OX
AND THE FROG

Two little Frogs were playing about at the edge of a pool when an Ox came down to the water to drink and by accident trod on one of them and crushed him. When the old Frog missed him, she asked his brother where he was. "He is dead, Mother," said the little Frog; "an enormous big creature with four legs came to our pool this morning and trampled him down in the mud."

"Enormous, was he? Was he as big as this?" said the Frog, puffing herself out to look as big as possible.

"Oh! Yes, yes, Mother, MUCH bigger," said the little Frog. And yet again she puffed and puffed herself out till she was almost as round as a ball.

"Cease, Mother, to puff yourself out," said the little Frog, "and do not be angry; for you would sooner burst then successfully imitate the hugeness of that creature."

Self-conceit may lead to self-destruction.

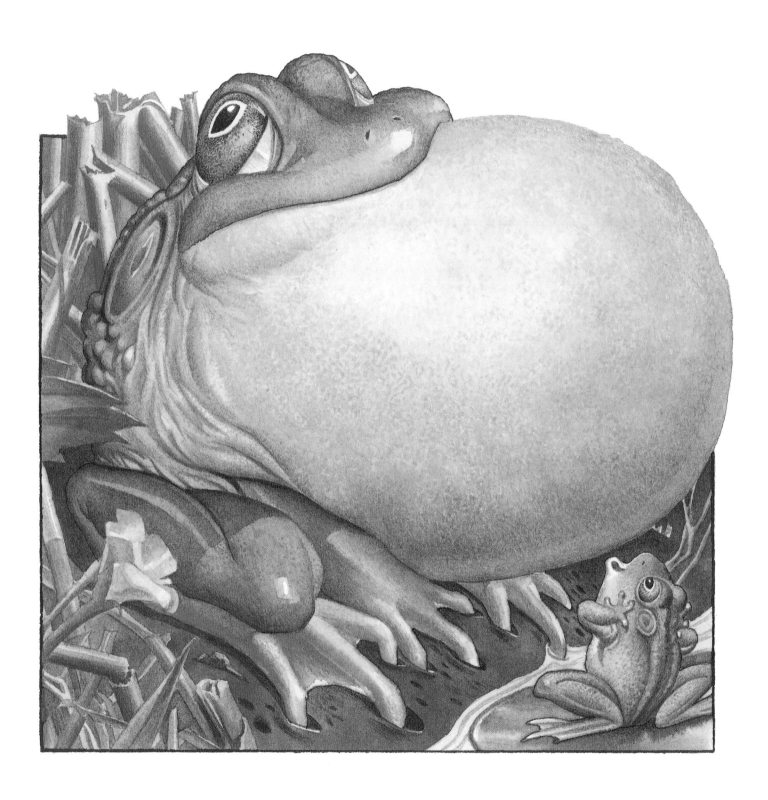

THE CRAB
AND HIS MOTHER

An Old Crab said to her son, "Why do you walk sideways like that, my son? You ought to walk straight."

The Young Crab replied, "Show me how, dear Mother, and I'll follow your example."

The Old Crab tried but tried in vain, and then saw how foolish she had been to find fault with her child.

Example is more powerful than precept.

THE HERON

A Heron went wading one early morning to take his breakfast from the shallows of a stream. There were many Fish in the water, but the stately Heron thought he could find better. "Such small fry is certainly not suitable fare for a Heron," he remarked to himself.

And as a choice young Perch swam by, the Heron tipped his long bill in the air and snapped, "No, sir, I certainly wouldn't open my beak for that!"

The sun grew higher and all the Fish left the shallows for the cool, deep, middle of the stream. When the Heron could find no trace of a Fish left in the stream, he was very grateful to finally break his fast on a mere snail.

Do not be too hard to suit or you may
have to be content with the worst or with nothing at all.

THE TOWN MOUSE
AND THE COUNTRY MOUSE

A Town Mouse and a Country Mouse were acquaintances, and the
Country Mouse one day invited his friend to come and see him
at his home in the fields. The Town Mouse came, and they sat down to
a dinner of barleycorns and roots, the latter of which had a distinctly
earthy flavor. The fare was not much to the taste of the guest, and
presently he broke out with, "My poor dear friend, you live here no
better than the ants. Now, you should just see how I fare! My larder is a
regular horn of plenty. You must come and stay with me, and I promise
you, you shall live on the fat of the land."

So when he returned to town he took the Country Mouse with him
and showed him a larder containing flour and oatmeal and figs and
honey and dates. The Country Mouse had never seen anything like it

and sat down to enjoy the luxuries his friend provided; but before they had begun, the door of the larder opened and someone came in. The two Mice scampered off and hid themselves in a narrow and exceedingly uncomfortable hole. Presently, when all was quiet, they ventured out again; but someone else came in, and off they scuttled again. This was too much for the visitor.

"Good-bye," said he, "I'm off. You live in the lap of luxury, I can see, but you are surrounded by dangers; whereas at home I can enjoy my simple dinner of roots and corn in peace."

Better a little in safety,
than an abundance surrounded by danger.

THE BEAR
AND THE BEES

A Bear was once searching for berries in the woods when he came across an old log where Bees had stored their honey. Wishing to find out whether the Bees were at home, he sniffed around the log with some caution. Along came a Bee on his way home from the fields with more honey, and on seeing the Bear, he angrily leapt upon his nose, stung him once, and flew swiftly into his house. The wretched Bear then rushed at the log with his teeth and claws, but the entire nest of Bees poured out and swarmed all over his body. Stumbling away in agony, the Bear was only able to save himself by falling headfirst into a nearby pond.

It is better to bear a single injury in silence
than to bring about a thousand by reacting in anger.

THE GRASSHOPPER
AND THE ANTS

One fine day in winter some Ants were busy drying their store of corn, which had got rather damp during a long spell of rain. Presently, up came a Grasshopper and begged them to spare her a few grains, "For," she said, "I'm simply starving."

The Ants stopped work for a moment, though this was against their principals. "May we ask," said they, "what you were doing with yourself all last summer? Why didn't you collect a store of food for the winter?"

"The fact is," replied the Grasshopper, "I was so busy singing that I hadn't the time."

"If you spent the summer singing," replied the Ants, "you can't do better than spend the winter dancing." And they went on with their work.

Idleness brings want.

THE GRASSHOPPER
AND THE OWL

An Owl, who lived in a hollow tree, was in the habit of feeding by night and sleeping by day; but her slumbers were greatly disturbed by the chirping of a Grasshopper, who had taken up his abode in the branches. She begged him repeatedly to have some consideration for her comfort, but the Grasshopper, if anything, only chirped the louder. At last the Owl could stand it no longer and was determined to rid herself of the pest by means of a trick. Addressing herself to the Grasshopper, she said in her most pleasant manner, "As I cannot sleep for your song, which, believe me, is as sweet as the sound of a harp, I have a mind to taste some nectar, which I was given the other day. Won't you come in and join me?"

The Grasshopper was flattered by the praise of his song, and his mouth, too, watered at the mention of the delicious drink, so he said he would be delighted. No sooner had he gotten inside the hollow where the Owl was sitting than she pounced upon him and ate him up.

Flattery is not proof of admiration.

THE HARE
AND THE TORTOISE

One day a Hare was making fun of a Tortoise for being so slow upon his feet. "Wait a bit," said the Tortoise, "I'll run a race with you, and I'll wager that I win."

"Oh, well," replied the Hare, who was much amused at the idea, "let's try and see," and it was soon agreed that the Fox should set a course for them and be the judge.

When the time came both started off together, but the Hare was soon so far ahead that he thought he might as well have a rest: so down he lay and fell fast asleep. Meanwhile the Tortoise kept plodding on and in time reached the goal. At last the Hare woke up with a start and dashed on at his fastest pace, but only to find that the Tortoise had already won the race.

Slow and steady wins the race.